Anonymous

Mr. Sweet Potatoes

And other stories

Anonymous

Mr. Sweet Potatoes
And other stories

ISBN/EAN: 9783744750400

Printed in Europe, USA, Canada, Australia, Japan

Cover: Foto ©Andreas Hilbeck / pixelio.de

More available books at **www.hansebooks.com**

MR.
SWEET POTATOES

AND OTHER STORIES

Illustrated

The Werner Company

NEW YORK   AKRON, OHIO   CHICAGO

1899

BREAKING THE CALVES.

MR. SWEET POTATOES.

OUR milkman has a very odd name, — translated into English it is " Sweet Potatoes." His Chinese neighbors call him " Old Father Sweet Potatoes."

Some persons think him a good man ; others say that he is a very bad one. Just how that is I do not know — his business brings him great temptation.

He is accused of putting water into the milk. He himself says, that he only does it when he has not enough milk to supply all his customers ; then he does not know what else he *can* do. When we engaged him to bring milk to us we took him into our yard and showed him that we had a well of our own.

The Chinese in their own country do not make any use of milk or butter. They have a perfect horror of cheese, and in this part of China, perhaps, not more than one man in a hundred will taste of beef. Only a few cows and bullocks are kept, and these are needed to plough the fields and turn the rude machinery of the sugar mills.

I suppose "Father Sweet Potatoes" had never thought of such a thing as owning a cow, until foreign ships began to come to his part of the country. Of course the ships brought foreign men and women, and these all wanted beef to eat — sometimes the Chinese, wishing to speak contemptuously of them, would call them "beef-eating foreigners," — and they also wanted milk for their cooking and for their children.

So Mr. Sweet Potatoes bought some cows, hoping to make some money in the milk business. They all had long ropes laced about their horns or threaded through their noses, and he got some little children to hold the ropes and guide the cows in search of food ; for there are no grass fields in this part of the country, and all the pastures the cows have are the little green places on the rocky hills and the grassy patches along the brooks ; and the children sit by and watch them while they graze, for there are no fences, and, left to themselves, the cows might stray into the rice fields or wander away into places where they would be stolen.

Mr. Sweet Potatoes.

Strange to say, we have our best milk when the winter has almost killed the grass, or when the weather is too stormy for the cows to go out; for then they are fed with the tops of pea-nut plants,

THE NATIVE HUMPBACK COW.

either green, or dried like hay, and up for sale in great bundles. This is delicious food for the cows, and when they have it then we have good milk indeed, with a thick, white cream upon it.

Sometimes they have cut grass to eat, which has

been brought from steep places on the hills to which the cows cannot go. Very poor boys go out with baskets and knives to gather this grass, and are paid only three or four cents for the work of a day.

Mr. Sweet Potatoes has two kinds of cows. Some of them are the native humpback cows, of very small size, very gentle; sometimes red and sometimes brown, with hair that is smooth and glossy quite down to the tiny little hoofs, which look far smaller and cleaner than do the feet of cows in colder climates where they walk out in snow and stand in frosty barns.

These cows have very small horns, sometimes three or four inches long, but often mere little white buds coming out from their dark foreheads. Back of their shoulders they have a small hump, three or four inches high. And, almost always, Sweet Potatoes' cows have with them a pretty, little, sprightly calf; for the Chinese believe, or pretend to believe, that if the calf were taken away the cow would die, and that it is necessary before milking her to first let the calf have a few mouthfuls of milk, — poor little calf!

The other cows are very different from these; they are water buffaloes, — buffaloes not at all like the shaggy bison, but great, awkward creatures, that in summer like to wade into pools, and, safe from flies and mosquitos, to stand with only their horns and upturned faces in sight above the top of the water; or, when there are no pools, to wander into bogs and half bury themselves in the mud. They are as large as a big ox, with very round bodies mounted on very slim legs that have very large knee and ankle joints. They are of the color of a mouse, or a gray pig, and coarse hairs grow thinly over their skin, while, in contrast to the humpback-cows, they have two immense, crescent-shaped horns setting up from their heads, and measuring often a yard from side to side.

Old Father Sweet Potatoes sells ten pint-bottles full for a silver dollar, — that is ten cents a pint,— and in summer he brings us a half-pint in the morning and another half-pint in the afternoon; for the weather is so hot that the milk of the morning will not remain sweet until evening, although the moment it is brought to the house it is boiled and then put in the coolest place we have, which is not a cellar, for cellars cannot be kept sweet and airy in countries where there is so much moisture and many insects.

When, in our walks, we meet these cows they often exhibit fear, especially of foreign ladies and horses, sights with which they are not familiar. The little humpback cows prance skittishly out of the paths; but the great buffaloes stand quite still and stare at us, then throw up their noses and sniff the air in an offended manner that in turn makes us afraid of them.

At night they are all brought home from their wanderings, and the ropes by which they are led are tied

THE WATER-BUFFALO.

to stakes driven into the ground ; in winter under a shed, but in summer in the open air. It makes one's neck ache to see them ; for the rope is frequently tied so short that they cannot hold their heads erect nor move them very freely, but they do not appear to suffer.

Next to his business the milkman values his daughter, who, when I first saw her, was a plump, rosy-cheeked child and tended her father's cows. If you ever saw a doll with a plaster head that had been broken and then had been mended by having a strip of black silk glued over the crack, you will know how Mr. Sweet Potatoes' daughter looked.

She wore a piece of black crape bound tightly about her head so that no one could see her hair. Some persons said that, owing to illness, she had no hair. If so it must have grown afterwards; for, when she was older and had left tending the cows, she had it put up on her head with pins, in a strange fashion that showed she was going to be married.

Sweet Potatoes had no son and he wished his son-in-law to come and live with him as if he belonged to him. Among the Chinese this is not considered so honorable or so genteel, as to have the daughter leave her home and go and live with her husband's family. It seemed strange that the son-in-law should consent; for though he was very poor he was also very proud, and was very particular to have respect shown to him and in regard to the kinds of work that he was willing to do. I should never have guessed his foolish reason for being so proud, but some one told me that it was because his father, now dead, had once held a small office in the Custom House!

SHETLAND WOMEN

NOT far outside the town of Lerwick, on the Shetland Islands there is a great, black, muddy tract of land called a peat-bog. All about is utter desolation. There are no huts even to be seen. The town is concealed by a rounded hill ; and when, through some opening between the bare upheavals, one catches a sight of the North Sea, it, too, seems deserted by mankind.

The peat, or mixture of roots and peculiar black soil, is dug here in large quantities ; and all about the place are great piles of it, dried and ready to be burned in the fire-places of the Lerwick people. Peat takes the place of wood ; and in every poor man's hut in Shetland will it be found burning brightly, and giving out a thin blue smoke.

To prepare peat for market, a great deal of labor is performed. First come the diggers — men, women and children. Entering upon the deep, miry bogs they cut the soil up into cakes about a foot long and a few inches thick , and these they place in high piles to dry. After a few weeks they come again, and carry the cured fuel away to the town.

It is while carrying these loads that the Shetlanders present a peculiar spectacle. The men are often very old, infirm and poorly clothed; and the women are dressed in short-skirted, home-spun gowns. below which may be seen very red and very broad feet. On their heads they usually have white caps, nicely ironed, with a fluted ruffle around the edge. Passing across the breast and over either shoulder are two strong straps, and these support an immense basket hanging against the back.

Thus equipped, the brave, stout women, their baskets piled with peat, tramp off to Lerwick, two miles away, to sell their loads for a few pennies each. They make many trips a day, always smiling, chatting and apparently contented. Often a long line may be seen carefully stepping along over the rough roads, stopping now and then to rest.

The homes of these poor peat women are, many of them, simply hovels. When they wish to build a

home, they go out into some fields, usually far away
from other huts, and there they dig a trench about a

SHETLAND WOMEN.

square piece of ground.   Upon this they build walls
to a height of about eight feet, and fill the crevices
with mud and bog.   For a roof they gather refuse

COAST OF SHETLAND

sea-wood, and, with this for a support, lay on layer after layer of straw. mud and stones.

But what homes they seem to us! There is no fire-place, only a hole in the ground, with a hole in the roof for the smoke to escape through! No windows, the door serving for both light and entrance! No beds, only heaps of straw! Sometimes in one small room, often the only one the house contains, will be seen man, wife, children, dog and hens, equal occupants, sharing the same rude comforts. Outside the house, if the owner be moderately well off, may be seen a herd of sheep or ponies, and a patch of garden surrounded by a wall.

But there is something a peat woman of Shetland is continually doing that we have not yet noticed. All have no doubt heard of Shetland hosiery; of the fine, warm shawls and hoods, and delicate veils that come from these far northern islands. Now, all the while the poor, bare-legged woman is carrying her heavy burden of peat, her hands are never idle. She is knitting, knitting away as fast as her nimble fingers will allow. In her pocket is the ball of yarn, and as her needles fly back and forth, she weaves fabrics of such fineness that the Royal ladies of England wear them; and no traveller visits the island without loading his

trunk with shawls, mittens, stockings, and other feminine fancies.

Not to know how to knit in Shetland is like not
knowing how to read at home. A little girl is taught
the art before she can read; and, as a result, at every
cottage will be found the spinning-wheel and the needles, while the feminine hands are never idle. It is
one great means of support; and on Regent Street
in London will be seen windows full of soft, white
goods marked " Shetland Hosiery."

Who first instructed these far northern people in this
delicate art is not surely known. On Fair Isle, one of
the Shetland group, the art is first said to have been
discovered, very many years ago. On that lonely isle
even now, every woman, girl and child knits while
working at any of her various duties.

The yarn with which the Shetland goods are made
is spun from the wool of the sheep we see roaming
about the fields. In almost every cottage may be
seen the veritable old-fashioned wheel ; and the busy
girl at the treadle sends the great wheel flying, and
spins out the long skeins, which serve to make baby
pretty hood or grandma a warm shawl.

MARDI GRAS IN NICE.

HAVE you ever happened in Nice at Carnival?

On a bright June morning, which my calendar called February twelfth, Rull and I tripped lightly down through the old olive orchards to the station, and billeted ourselves for Nice.

Long before we reached Nice Rull's hands tingled; for there lay a beautiful line of snow, miles away, on the *north* side of the Alps, and the poor fellow hadn't been as near a snow-ball as that for the winter. But I had only to say "*confetti!*" and his eyes danced at the vision of the parti-colored hailstorm to come.

Now hasten with us at once to the *Promenade du Cours*, up and down which the procession is to pass.

First, however, I shall buy for you each a little blue gauze mask ; for you cannot even peep at Carnival unmasked. And if any of you can wear linen dusters with hoods attached, all the better. Don't

"PROMENADE DU COURS," IN CARNIVAL TIME.

leave a square inch of skin unprotected, I warn you.

Besides the little masks, you may buy, each of you, a whole bushel of these "sugar-plums," and have them sent to our balcony. Also for each a little tin scoop fastened on a flexible handle, which you are to fill with *confetti* but on no account to pull — at least, not yet.

The crowds are gathering. Pretty peasant girls in their holiday attire of bright petticoats, laced bodices, and white frilled caps; stray dominoes; richly dressed ladies with mask in hand; carriages so decorated with flowers as to be artistically hidden — even the wheels covered with batiste — blue, pink, purple, green or buff. Even the sidewalk, as we

"PROMENADE DU COURS" IN CARNIVAL TIME.

pass, is fringed with chairs at a franc each.

The " *Cours* " is gay with suspended banners, bright with festooned balconies and merry faces. Sidewalks and street are filled with people; but the horses have the right of way, and the people are fined if they are run over.

Let us hasten to our balcony, for here passes a

band of musicians, in scarlet and gold, to open the procession.

Just in time we take our seats, and lo! before us rolls a huge car.

It is "the theatre" — an open car of puppets — but the puppets are *men;* all attached to cords held in the hand of the giant, who sits in imposing state

"PROMENADE DU COURS," IN CARNIVAL TIME.

above them on the top of the car which is on a level with the third story balconies.

The giant lifts his hand and the puppets whirl and jump. But alas! his head is too high. His hat is swept off by the hanging festoons, and the giant must ride bare-headed, in danger of sunstroke.

Next behind the car moves in military order a

regiment of mounted grasshoppers. Their sleek, shining bodies of green satin, their gauzy wings and antennæ, snub noses and big eyes, are all absolutely perfect to the eye ; but — they are of the size of men.

You lower your mask to see more clearly, you are lost in wonder at the perfect illusion, your mouth is wide open with "Ohs !" and "Ahs !" when *pop !*

" PROMENADE DU COURS" IN CARNIVAL TIME.

pop ! slings a shower of *confetti*, and the little hailstones seem to cut off your ears and rush sifting down your neck.

For, while you were watching the grasshoppers, a low open carriage, concealed under a pink and white cover, has stopped under our windows. Four merry masqueraders, cloaked and hooded in hue to match, have a bushel of *confetti* between them, and are piled with nosegays. We slink behind our masks, we pull the handles of our *confetti* scoops — then the battle begins and waxes fierce.

But they are crowded on; for behind them, in irresistible stateliness, moves on the Sun and Moon. Then come the Seasons: Winter represented by a

" PROMENADE DU COURS," IN CARNIVAL TIME.

band of Russians, fur-covered from top to toe, dragging a Siberian sledge. Summer is recognized by a car-load of choicest flowers, whose fragrance reaches us as they pass.

Here rolls a huge wine cask which fills half the wide street; there moves a pine cone, six feet high, to the eye perfectly like the cones, six inches in length, which we use daily to light our olive-wood fire.

Then a procession of giant tulips — stalk, calyx, petals, all complete. They also silently move on.

Next a huge pot, with a cat climbing its side, her paw just thrust beneath the lid. Ha! it suddenly flies off. Does the cat enter? We cannot see through the crowd. A colossal stump follows, trail-

"PROMENADE DU COURS," IN CARNIVAL TIME.

ing with mosses and vines. Upon it a bird's nest filled with young, their mouths wide open for food; wonderful, because the artistic skill is so perfect that, although so immense, they seem living and not unnatural.

Then a car of Arctic bears champing to and fro in the heat, poor things, as well they may ; for this is cloudless sky and an Italian sun. Look carefully at them and tell me, are they not true bears?

But ah! *sling! sling!* two handfuls of *confetti* sting your eyes back into place again, and dash the bears out of sight. Isn't it delightfully unbearable? You shout at the folly of having forgotten *confetti,* and then resolve to watch your chance at the next poor

" PROMENADE DU COURS " IN CARNIVAL TIME.

foot-pad.

Here passes a man with two faces. His arms are neatly folded before, also behind. You cannot tell which is the real front, until, suddenly, a horse trots up and nearly touches noses, while the man moves on undisturbed. You meant to give that man a dash, but you forgot, he was so queer.

Ah! here comes a carriage of pretty girls. Down pours the shot from the balcony above. It rains on you like hail. It runs in rills down your back. You hold your recovered ears, and add your tone to the rippling, rippling laughter that flows on in silvery tide.

Not one boisterous shout, not one impatient excla-

" PROMENADE DU COURS " IN CARNIVAL TIME.

mation the whole livelong day ; only everywhere the sound of childish glee. How good to see even old careworn faces lighted up with mirth !

Here goes an ostrich with a monkey on his back then a man with a whole suit of clothes neatly fitted out of Journals.

But — look ! look ! there towers a huge car. Nay,

It is a basket — a vegetable basket! but its sides are
as high as our balcony. On its corners stand white
carrots with their green waving tops upward.
Around the edges are piled a variety of garden beau-
ties.

But, wonderful to see, in the centre rises a mammoth cabbage. Its large-veined petals are as perfect
as any you ever saw in your garden, but their tips
reach above the third balcony. Upon these veined
petals climb gorgeous butterflies, whose wings slowly
shut and open while they sip. As the mammoth
passes, the outer petals slowly droop, and snails are
seen clinging within, while gayly-hued butterflies
creep into view.

Now the carriages mingle gayly in the procession.
Here is one with young lads, their faces protected
with gauze masks, which laughably show shut red
lips without, and two red lines of lips and white glittering teeth within. The battle of *confetti* waxes hot.
Merry faces fill all balconies and windows. Many a
beauty drops her mask for an instant like ourselves
to peer more eagerly at the wonderful procession, but
at her peril. On the instant *dash! dash!* flies the
confetti, slung with force enough from the little scoops
to sting sharply.

War is the fiercest yonder where there is such a

handsome family (Americans we are sure), father, mother and daughter.

Here goes a carriage decorated with United States flags ; all its occupants cloaked and hooded in gray linen, the carriage covered likewise. They stop beneath the balcony, and *sling! sling! sling!* in wildest combat until crowded on.

Up and down the procession sweeps. Up one side the wide " *Cours* " and down the other ; the space within filled with the merry surging crowd, under the feet of the horses it would seem. But no matter. Horses and men and women and children bear a charmed life to-day.

Now and then a policeman pounces on the boys, who are gathering up the heaps of *confetti* from the dirt to sell again ; but this is the only suggestion of law and order behind the gay confusion.

Here rolls a carriage trimmed with red and white. Within are a pair of scarlet dominoes, who peer mysteriously at you.

But look again at what moves on. A car longer than any yet seen.

It is a grotto. Within its cool recesses bask immense lizards. Some slowly climb its sides, then, in search of prey, thrust out their long tongues. In shining coat, in color, in movement, you would avow them to be lizards, truly. But how huge!

Behind the lizards pass again the mounted grass-hoppers, our favorites of all, for their wonderfully perfect form and dainty beauty. And lo! they bear, to our delight, a silken banner, token of the prize.

For, pets, do you read between the lines and understand that this wonderful procession was the result of truly artistic skill? — that to imitate perfectly to the eye, to represent exactly in motion all these living creatures, and yet conceal within a boy or man who invisibly moved them, required all the delicacy of perception and nicety of workmanship of French eyes and fingers? Think you that your little fingers and bright eyes will ever attain so much.

Besides, all this was also a great outlay of thousands of francs. For Nice aroused herself to excel in Carnival, and offered large prizes — one of five thousand francs, another of four, another of three — for the most perfect representations.

Nowhere in Italy was there anything to compare with Nice. And I doubt if you would see again in Carnival what would so perfectly delight your young eyes, or so quicken your perception of artistic skill.

We look at our watches. Two hours yet; but we long to taste the fun on foot. So we fling our last *confetti*, fill hair and button-holes and hands with our sweet nosegays of geranium, sweet alyssum, mignonette and pansies — mementoes of the fight, — then descend to the sidewalk to press our way along the crowded court.

More and more to see! and, last of all, Carnival tossed and tumbled in effigy until his death by drowning or burning.

But we must be early at the station. Early, indeed! Peppered and pelted all the way, tweaked and shot at; but ever and always with *only* the harmless *confetti* and soft nosegays.

Sure that we are the first to leave, sure that no others are there before us, we pass into the outer baggage-room. Fifty more are there pressed hard against the closed door.

The crowd swells; hundreds are behind us; we can scarcely keep our feet. Yet what a good-natured crowd! The hour for the train to leave passes. By and by the closed door opens a crack; a gilt-banded arm is thrust through and *one* person taken out, and the solemn door closed again.

So, one by one, we ooze through, pass the turnstile in the passage under surveillance of the keen-eyed officer, and are admitted into the saloon, which is also locked.

We sink down into a seat nearest *the* one of two doors which instinct tells us is to be opened. Again we wait an hour till the last panting victim is passed through the stile.

Then, O! it is not our door which unlocks and opens but the other. We rush for a compartment; but no! all appear filled, so we step to an official and state our case.

He conducts us on, on, nearly to the end of the train, over stones and timbers; but, at last, bestows us out of that crowd in a compartment with but three persons. Soon we leave, only two hours later than the time advertised.

For in France, little pets, the trains wait for the people. The people are locked in till all is ready; then follows a rush like a grand game of "puss, puss in the corner!" and almost always there is some poor puss who cannot get in.

Guess how many bushels of *confetti* rattled on the floor of our chamber that night!

ON THE FARM IN WINTER.

THE life of a boy in winter on the old-fashioned New England farm seems to me one of the best of the right kinds of life for a healthy lad, provided his tastes have not been spoiled by wrong reading, or by some misleading glimpse of a city by gas-light. It certainly abounds with the blood and muscle-making sports for which the city physiologists so anxiously strive to substitute rinks and gymnasiums.

But I rather pity a young fellow who gets his only sleigh rides by paying a dollar an hour to the livery-stable, and who must do his skating within limits on artificial ice. He never gets even a taste of such primitive fun as two boys I know had last winter. The sleigh was at the wagon-maker's shop for repairs when the first heavy snow fell, and they harnessed

Dobbin to an old boat, and had an uproarious ride up hill and down dale, with glorious bumps and jolts.

I rather pity a fellow, too, who eats grocer's apples, and confectioner's nuts, and baker's cream cakes, who never knows the fun of going down cellar to the apple bins to fill his pockets for school, and who owns no right in a pile of butternuts on the garret floor. I am sorry for a boy that knows nothing of the manly freedom of trowsers tucked in boots, hands and feet both cased in home-knit mittens and home-knit socks — I cannot believe his blood is as red, or can possibly flow so deep and strong in his side-walk sort of life, as the young fellows who chop wood and ply the snow-shovel, and turn out *en masse* with snow-ploughs after a long storm — the sound of the future strength of the land is in the sturdy stamp of their snowy boots at the door as they come in from their hearty work. I am not writing of country boys that want to be clerks, — they are spoiled for fun anyhow, — but of the boys that expect, if they expect anything in particular, to stay on the farm and own it themselves some day.

This stinging cold morning the boys at the schoolhouse door are not discussing the play-bills of the *Globe* or the *Museum*, but how the river froze last night, turning the long quiet surface to blue-black ice, as smooth as a looking-glass. Now what skating ! what grand noonings, what glorious evenings ! No rink or frog-pond, where one no sooner gets under headway than he must turn about, but miles and miles of curving reaches leading him forward between rustling sedges, till he sees the white caps of the open lake dancing before him.

Presently the snow comes and puts an end to the sport; for sweeping miles and miles of ice is out of the question. After the snow, a thaw; and then the jolly snow-balling. There is not enough of a thaw to take the snow off; only enough to make it just sufficiently sloppy and soft for the freeze-up that follows to give it a crust almost as hard and smooth as the ice lately covered up.

Then such coasting ! Just think of dragging your sled of a moonlight night up a mile of easy tramping to the foot of the mountain, whence you come down again, now fast, now slow, now "like a streak" down a sharp incline, now running over a even-rail fence buried in the glittering drifts, and bringing up at last at a neighbor's door, or at the back side of your own barnyard!

It is great fun, too, to slide on the drifts with "slews" or "jump- ers." These are made sometimes of one, sometimes of two barrel-staves, and are sure to give you many a jolly bump and wintersault.

There is fun to be had *in* the drifts too, digging caves or under-snow houses, wherein you may build a fire without the least danger. Here you can be Esquimaux, and your whole tribe sally forth from the igloë and attack a terrible white bear, if one of the party will kindly consent to be a bear for awhile. You can make him white enough by pelting him with snow, and he will *bear* enough before he is finally killed.

There is fun, too, and of no mean order, to be got out of the regular farm duties. Not much, per-haps, out of bringing in the wood, or feeding the pigs, or turning the fanning-mill; but foddering the sheep and calves, which, very likely, are pets, takes the boys to the hay-mow, where odors of summer linger in the herds-grass, and the daisy and clover-tops are almost as green and white and

THE IMPROVISED SLEIGH

yellow and purple as when they fell before the scythe.

What a place is this elastic floor for a "wrestle or a summersault!" and then, who "da's't" climb to the big beam, into the neighborhood of the empty swallows nests and dusty cobwebs, and take the flying jump therefrom to the mow? Here, too, are hens' nests to be found, with frost-cracked eggs to carry in rats, and larger prey, also to be hunted when the hay is so nearly spent that the fork sticks into the loose boards at the bottom of the hay.

But of all things which the farmer's boy is wanted to do, and wants to do, there is nothing such clear fun as the breaking of a yoke of calves. First, the little yoke is to be got on to the pair somehow and a rope made fast to the "nigh" one's head, that is, the calf on the left side, where the driver goes. Then comes bawling and hauling and pushing, and often too much beating, until the little cattle are made to understand that "Gee" means turn to the right, and "Haw" means turn to the left, and that "Whoa" means stop, and "Back" means, of them all, just what is said.

Every command is roared and shouted; for an

idea seems to prevail that oxen, big and little, are deaf as adders, and can never be made to hear except at the top of the voice. In a still, winter day, you may hear a grown-up ox-teamster roaring at his patient beasts two miles away; and a calf-breaker not half his size may be heard more than half as far. Then, on some frosty Saturday, when the little nubby-horned fellows have learned their lessons, they are hitched to a sled, and made to haul light loads, a little wood, or some of the boys,— the driver still holding to the rope, and flourishing his whip as grand as a drum-major.

Once in a while the little oxen of the future take matters into their own hoofs and make a strike for freedom, upsetting the sled and scattering its load, and dragging their driver headlong through the snow.

But they have to submit at last; and three or four years hence, you would never think from their solemn looks and sober pace that they ever had thought of such rebellious freaks. They were the boy's calves, but father's oxen.

Halter-breaking a colt is almost as good as breaking steers, only there is no sled-riding to be had in this.

UPON THE HAY-MOW.

Till lately, the young fellow has had the freedom of the fields, digging in the first snows for a part of his living, and with his rough life has grown as shaggy-coated as a Shetland pony, with as many burrs stuck in his short foretop as it will hold; for if there is an overlooked burdock on all the farm, every one of the horse kind running at large will find it, and each get more than his share of burrs matted and twisted into his foretop and mane.

Now, he is waxed and driven into a shed or stable, and fooled or forced to put his head into a long, stout, rope halter. Then he is got into the clear, open meadow, and his first lesson begins. The boys all lay hold of the rope at a safe distance from the astonished pupil, and pull steadily upon him. Just now he would rather go any way than straight ahead, and holds back with all his might, looking, with all his legs braced forward, his neck stretched to its utmost, and his head on a line with it, like a stubborn little donkey who has lost something in ears, but nothing in willfulness, and gained a little in tail. At last he yields a little to the uncomfortable strain, and takes a few reluctant steps forward, then rears and plunges and throws himself, and is drawn struggling headlong through the snow, until he tires of such rough usage and flounders to his feet.

Then he repeats his bracing tactics, the boys bracing as stoutly against him, till he suddenly gives way and they go tumbling all in a heap.

If the boys tire out before the colt gives up, there are other days coming, and sooner or later he submits; and in part compensation for not having his own way, he has a warm stall in the barn, and eats from a manger, just like a big horse, and is petted and fondled, and grows to be great friends with his young masters — at last to be "father's horse," instead of " our colt."

But by and by the long winter — this play-day of the year for the farm-boy — comes to an end, to make way for spring — spring which brings to him work out of all reasonable proportion to the amount of play, at least so the farm-boy is likely to think.

A CHINAMAN'S QUEUE.

EVERYONE knows that a Chinaman wears his hair in a queue, but not every· one knows why he does so. A China- man's queue is not a mere oddity or variety; it is, to him, a very serious thing ; losing it, he would almost sell his respectability, and history tells of more than one time when it has been a matter of life and death.

In many of their customs the people of China fol- low their forefathers of more than a thousand years ago, but queues may be called a new fashion, having only been worn about two hundred and fifty years.

In very old times, the Chinese wore their long hair put up in a peculiar manner upon the tops of their heads, and called themselves "The Black-Haired Race;" but about the time that the Pilgrims landed at Plymouth, in the year 1627, the Tartars, who had come down from Manchuria, and, after long wars, had conquered China, which they have governed ever since, made a law that all the Chinese, to show that they had been conquered, should take down their top-knots, and wear their hair as the Tartars did, in a hanging braid; and they threatened to kill all who would not do it.

Of course the Chinese were greatly distressed by this; but, as it was better to have a tail than to be without a head, they submitted in the end, making the best of what they could not help.

The people of southern China held out longest against the queue, and, in one district, men were hired to wear it. Even now, dwelling among the hills, are a few men belonging to a very old and wild tribe, whose pride it is that they have never worn hanging hair; while the Amoy men, who were the very last to yield to the Tartars, wear a turban to hide the shaven head, and the detested tail; but some persons think that the nation in general have come to like the new style better that the old ; others think that they would gladly go back to the old way, if they could.

A few years ago there was a great rebellion in China. A part of the Chinese rebelled against the Tartars, and all the rebels put up their hair in the old Chinese fashion ; and, because they did not shave their heads, they went by the name of the " Long-Haired Robbers." When any of their soldiers met a man with a queue they knew that he was loyal to the Tartar government, and they would kill him, or cut off his queue, or do what they liked with him ; and, on the other hand, the life of a " Long-Haired Robber " was not safe for a moment if he fell into the hands of the government troops. At length, after many, many millions of people were killed, queues carried the day, and the rebels were conquered.

I have heard that thieves sometimes have their queues cut off for a punishment, and, now and then, I suppose, a person's hair must fall off after illness, but, in these cases, it would grow again.

There are two classes of men in China who never wear queues — the Buddhist priests, who shave their heads all over, and who can be known by the color of their gowns, and their queer hats, and the Tauists, who, as a sign of their priesthood, wear their hair in a kind of twist on the back of their heads. With these few exceptions, every Chinaman has a queue, from the young child whose short hairs are pinched up, sometimes on the crown of the head, and sometimes on the sides of it, and braided with threads of red silk into a tight little tail a few inches long, so stiff that it stands straight out from the head, up to the almost bald old man, whose straggling gray hairs are tied into a thin wisp at the back of his neck.

The Chinese have usually a good quantity of hair, coarse, perfectly straight, and jetty black, except, in a few cases, where, from illness, the color is rusty black. They have hardly any beard, but some of them — though not often before they are grandfathers, and more than forty years old — wear a much-admired moustache. Accustomed to black locks and smooth faces, they look curiously on the full beards of the men, and the yellow curls of the children, of our fairer race, or, as they style us, "The Red-Headed Foreigners."

The Chinese shave the whole head, except a round patch on the crown, about as large as a breakfast saucer. On this they let the hair grow, and it is combed back and down, and tied firmly with a string, at the middle of the bottom of the patch. It is then divided into three strands and braided. If a man is very poor, he simply has a plat, the length of his hair, fastened at the end with a cotton string ; but the Chinese have a good deal of pride about their hair, and, if they can afford it, like to have the queue handsomely made. Often tresses of false hair are added to it, for making which the hairs that fall out are carefully saved. Of course, the hair is thinner at the end than at the top, and to keep the braid of more even size, and to increase its length, long bunches of black silk cord are gradually woven into it.

Queues vary in length, but grown men often wear them hanging nearly to their shoes, the upper part of the braid being of hair, and the lower part of black silk cord, which is tied in a tassel at the end. In southern China, children's queues are made bright and jaunty with crimson silk.

For mourning white cord is used, and for half mourning blue. Also, persons in mourning do not have their heads shaven for a certain length of time. When the emperor dies, nobody in China is expected to be shaven for one hundred days.

Commonly, tidy, well-to-do people have their heads shaven every few days, and, as no one could easily shave the top of his own head, everybody employs a barber. Of course there are a great many barbers, and, with all the millions of people in China, they have a large business.

Besides the shops, many barbers have little mova-ble stands containing all their tools, and they may of-ten be seen plying their art by the wayside, or at the houses of their customers. The barber has a basin of hot water, a towel, and an awkward kind of razor; and when he has shaven and washed the head, and braided the hair of a man, he ends up all by patting him, with both hands, upon the back and shoulders, in a way which, to him, is truly delightful. For all this, his charge is not more than six cents, and a poor man would pay still less.

To make his queue thicker, sometimes a Chinaman wishes to grow more hair, and the barber will leave his head unshaven for, perhaps, a quarter of an inch all round the old circle of hair. When the new hair is an inch or two long, being very stiff, it stands up in a fringe — like a kind of black halo — all round his head, looking very comically, and annoying the China-man very much, until it is long enough to be put into the braid.

When a man is at work, he finds his queue very much in his way, and he binds it about his head, or winds it up in a ball behind, where he sometimes fast-ens it with a small wooden comb; but, in his own country, on all occasions of form and dress, he wears it hanging, and it would not be polite to do otherwise.

11

As it would take a long time to dry it, he dislikes to wet it, and, if rain comes on, hastens to roll it up and cover it.

Sometimes beggars, to make themselves look very wretched, do not dress their hair for a long time, and it becomes so frizzed and matted that hardly anything could be done to it, but to cut most of it off.

When a culprit is arrested in China, the officer takes hold of his queue and leads him to prison by it, often treating him very cruelly.

Little girls, as well as little boys, have their heads shaven when they are about a month old. This is done before an idol, with a good deal of parade. Young girls also wear their hair in queues, but as when older their heads are not shaven like those of the boys, a larger quantity of hair is drawn back into the braid, making it much heavier. When married their hair is put up in the fashion of the women of the district where they live, but married women never wear their hair braided.

One who has lived long in China does not like to see a thin, uneven queue, tied with a cotton string; it has a slovenly, poverty-stricken air; while a thick, glossy braid, with a heavy bunch of silk in the end of it, looks tidy and prosperous; and a neat plat of sil-very hair betokens comfortable old age.

MEXICAN WATER-CARRIERS

A MEXICAN water-carrier is always an oddly-dressed fellow. He looks something like the man some one met "one misty, moisty morning," who was all clothed in leather. He has a leather cap, jacket and trousers, the last reaching only to his knees, and held aside with bright buttons of silver, so as to show the white cotton drawers beneath. Down the front of his jacket, too, and around the rim of his cap, are bright buttons. Fastened at his side is a leather wallet holding his money. On his feet are leather sandals. Over his head are two stout leather straps, holding two jugs of earthernware, one

ALWAYS ON A LITTLE INDIAN TROT.

resting on his back and the other hanging in front.

He begins work early in the morning. If you go into any of the public squares in the city of Mexico, you will then see a great many of them all seated around the stone basin and busy preparing for the day's work. They reach far over the edge and, dipping up the water, fill their large jug. Throwing that on their backs they reach down once more and fill the smaller one, and then trot off and visit the different houses of the city, and sell the families what water they want.

You would say, perhaps, it was a heavy load to carry by the head and neck, but the carrier does not seem to mind it, for he is very strong, and the jugs just balance each other. It is said an Englishman was once told of this balance, and, to see if it were so, he waited until a carrier came along and then, with his cane, broke one of the jugs. Alas! down came the man, jugs and all ; his balance surely was gone.

Water has to be brought about in this manner because none runs into the houses by lead pipes, as with us. It all comes from near the old castle of Chapultepec, three or four miles from the city.

It runs over great stone aqueducts, built by Cortes, and when it reaches the public square falls into the stone basins of the city. So, you see, it makes these carriers almost like our milkmen, only they do not come with a fine horse and carriage, and do not make nearly as much money. They only get a few cents each day. How hard they work, too! Busy from morn till eve, always earnest, hardly ever smiling, always on a little Indian trot, they go about from house to house, and then, when the day's work is over, what a life they lead !

They have no home to go to, either ; they live in the streets, sleep in the gutter or on the cathedral stone steps, and often, I fear, get so befogged on "pulque," the national drink, that they care not whether they have a home and good bed or not.

Think what a miserable existence, not knowing how to read, dressing as those before them did three hundred years ago, and doing nothing but carrying water about the city. Every day they will go into the great cathedral and say their prayers. They put their jugs down beside them, clasp their hands, raise their eyes to the image of their patron saint, and mumble their requests or their thanks, and then, taking a last look at the gold candlesticks and rich ornaments, will hurry away, and continue their hard, uninteresting daily labors.

A VERY QUEER HOUSE.

THERE are few pleasanter places in summer than the great square of Et-Meidaun at Constantinople. The tall gray pointed monument in the middle, like a sentry watching over the whole place, the white houses along either side, the polished pavement, the high white walls and rounded domes, and tall slender towers and cool shadowy gateways of the Turkish mosques together with the bright blue sky overhead and the bright blue sea in the distance below, make a very pretty picture indeed.

The different people, too, that go past us are quite a show in themselves. Now, it is a Turkish soldier in blue frock and red cap — a fine tall fellow, but rather thin and pale, as if he did not always get enough to eat; now, a tall, dark, grave-looking American, with a high funnel-shaped hat, and a long black frock right down to his feet. There comes a big, jolly-looking English sailor, rolling himself along with his hands in his pockets and his hat on one side. There goes a Russian with a broad flat face and thick yellow beard. That tall handsome man in the laced jacket and black velvet trousers, who is looking after him so fiercely, is a Circassian, who was fighting against the Russians among the mountains of the Caucasus not many years ago. And behind him is an Arab water-carrier, with limbs bare to the knee and a huge skin bag full of water on his back.

But the strangest sight of all is still to come.

Halting to look around I suddenly espy a pair of yellow Turkish slippers, a good deal worn, lying at the foot of a huge tree which stands alone in the midst of the open space. They are not flung carelessly down, either, as if their owner had thrown them away, but placed neatly side by side; just as an orderly old gentleman might put *his* slippers beside the fire before going out. And, stranger still, although at least half a dozen bare-footed Turks (who might think even an old shoe worth picking up) have passed by and seen them, not one of them has ventured to disturb them in any way.

My Greek companion notices my surprise, and gives a knowing grin, like a man who has just asked you a riddle which he is sure you will never guess.

"Aha, Effendi! Don't you think he must have been a careless fellow who left his slippers there? See anything odd about this tree?"

"Nothing but that piece of board on it which I suppose covers a hollow."

"That's just it!" chuckles the Greek. "It covers a *hollow*, sure enough — look here, Effendi!"

He taps thrice upon the "piece of board," which suddenly swings back like a door, disclosing to my astonished eyes, in the dark hollow, the long blue robe, white turban, and flowing beard of an old Turk.

"Peace be with you!" says the old gentleman in a deep hoarse voice, nodding to my companion, whom he seems to know.

"With you be peace," answers the Greek. "You didn't expect that, did you, Effendi? It's not every day that you find a man living inside a tree?"

"*Does* he live here, then?"

"To be sure he does. Didn't you see his slippers at the door? Nobody would touch the slippers for any money. They all know old Selim. He has a snug house, after all ; and don't pay *rent* either l"

In truth, the little place is snug enough, and certainly holds a good deal for its size. On one side is an earthen water-jar, on the other a huge blanket-like cloak, which probably represents Mr. Selim's whole stock of bedding. A copper stew-pan is fixed to a spike driven into the wood, while just above it a small iron funnel, neatly fitted into a knot-hole of the trunk, does duty as a chimney. Around the sides of the hollow hang a long pipe, a tobacco-pouch, a leathern wallet, and some other articles, all bearing marks of long service ; while to crown all, my guide shows me, triumphantly, just outside the door, a wooden shelf with several pots of flowers — a garden that just matches the house.

Having given us this sight of his house-keeping, the old gentleman (who has been standing like a statue during the whole inspection) silently holds out his hand. I drop into it a double piastre (ten cents) and take my leave, reflecting that if it is good to be content with little this old hermit is certainly a bit of a hero in his way.

IN BELGIUM.

AFTER rolling and tossing for twenty-four hours upon the German Ocean, the sight of land should be hailed with a spirit of thankfulness. But of all inhospitable shores, those of the Belgian coast, in the month of November, must carry the palm. The waters, gray and rough, dash upon a sandy beach for miles and miles, showing no signs of life, if we except an occasional wind-mill in action. Row after row of poplar trees form a partial back-ground. Somewhat stripped of their leaves, they have the appearance of so many gray pillars holding up the sky.

As the low-built towns with their red houses rise to view, and the dikes present themselves, if this be the first introduction into Continental Europe, the foreignness stands out in bold relief. But as you ascend the river the villages are more interesting and indications of life more frequent. Long before reaching the pier at Antwerp, its towers salute the travellers, and the gratitude becomes apparent on each and every visage.

Our little windows in the above-mentioned city overlooked its prettiest park, in the centre ot which stands the statue of Rubens. At the right, yet full in view, stands the Cathedral of Notre Dame, famous for its ninety-nine bells (why not one more?) and the masterpieces of the great artist of Antwerp.

Of these paintings, the "Assumption," which has within a comparatively short time been restored, is truly beautiful, the countenances of the several figures wearing a pure expression, which is not a characteristic of the Rubens face in general. The fame of the others is perhaps yet greater than that of the "Assumption," and everywhere in our own country are engravings and photographs of the same, on exhibition or in private collections. Before these the lover of art lingers to study, and studying continues to linger. For me, alas! these *chef d'œuvres*, "The Ascent to the Cross" and the "The Descent from the Cross," have no attractions.

The music of the bells at sunset repays one, not only for the tumble of the German Sea, but for the voyage across the Atlantic, especially in the autumn, when the twilights are so short that the Mall is lightest as the sun goes down. This music singularly contrasts with the noise made by the footfall of the peasants. This numerous class, hurrying home at dusk, take the park as their shorter course. The click-clack of the hundreds of wooden shoes of all sizes and intensities, rapidly "getting by," is something that can never be imagined. As these articles of apparel are seldom of a snug fit in the region of the heel, there is a peculiar introduction to each grand step. The quantity and quality of this noise are astonishing; the novelty, a charm.

There is one sound, however, which is sensibly wanting among the lower class of Belgians. It may never have been in the experience of others, but it could not be entirely my own imagination — I missed the human voice in the groups of peasantry. The uneducated of other countries have at least a common "mongrel tongue" to some extent, but the individual vocabulary of this class is certainly very limited, which is a check to prolonged conversation. This feature was to me a cause satisfactory for the stillness of the streets, thronged as they sometimes are, and may be the reason that the foot-fall is so impressive, with its wooden encumbrances.

Next to the shoe, the attraction was the harnessed dogs and the young girls drawing burdens.

When a woman was seen wheeling a cart or trundling a barrow, it was just to conclude that she was in the interest of her own gain, and we could pass on. When the dogs, the old and despised of their kind, were leisurely carrying their wagon of vegetables, provided the driver was kind, it was rather a foreign sight than a painful one. Often these dogs lie down in the harness—the latter not being very elaborate — and do not seem unwilling to rise to the occasion. When it happened, as often it did, during our short sojourn in Belgium, that we saw girls, the young and bright and strong, bearing these burdens, frequently sharing the harness with the aforesaid animals, the American heart rebelled. If they were rough, hoydenish girls, romping all day long, filling their carts with sand for the fun and having a boy-companion as a play-driver, we should even then think, do they *never* go to school?

But they were not of this class! They were the quiet and obedient, generally tidy in appearance, calmly accepting their lot in life through ignorance. I never saw a boy thus disgraced ; not that I feel less glad for " him," but the more sad for " her."

When walking one day, having lost my way, I met

one of these teams. There were connected with it two young girls, about fifteen years of age — one harnessed and drawing the load, the other having the charge of the cargo, which, from its too great abundance, required constant diligence. I inquired of them the direction to the hotel.

Without altering a muscle, they continued their gaze (we had begun the stare from afar). So listless was it that they seemed like pet animals, who look at one confidingly, except in the case of the latter there will be "wink of recognition." No attempt was made to reply. After I turned, they kept their eyes upon the space which I had occupied, as if I had merely been an obstruction to their sunshine. A person, not far from them, answered my inquiries, adding, with a nod towards the "little workers," "they only talk mongrel."

This woman, short and chubby, forcibly reminded me of somebody or something in the past. After a brief reflection, behold the solution:

Before toys had become so elaborate in our own country, there occasionally found their way from Holland images of pewter, representing the dairymaids of that part of Europe. They were far different from the pewter-pieces of the present day, being thicker and less destructible. The one that came into my possession, the delight of my heart, wore the short, full dress and sun-bonnet, with arms akimbo. The one, ah me! that would have been my choice was purchased by a class-mate, she having at that time, and I presume at this time, twice my amount of funds. The price of this precious bit was two cents.

The latter figure, unlike mine, had the pail poised upon the head. It was probably a true likeness of the renowned maid that counted the chickens in advance, thereby showing the people of her country to have been "born calculators.' I think the little body that showed me the way to my lodgings descended in a direct line from this old mathematical stock, and was a little proud of her origin. Her language was a mixture of Dutch, French, and, for all I know, several dead languages, *but* — and I have her own authority for it — not a mongrel tongue. Out of gratitude to one who led me to my home, I should speak well of this woman, as of the proverbial bridge, so am quite willing to accept her statement and allow her a "pure dialect."

JOE THE CHIMPANZEE.

WHEN in England I was very much interested
in the monkeys at the Zoological Gardens,
Regent's Park, London. There were hundreds of
all kinds and sizes, from the gigantic orang-outang
to tiny creatures not much bigger than a large rat.

These monkeys had a spacious glass house, heat-
ed by steam ; and as a tropical temperature was always maintained, tall palms and luxurious vines grew
so vigorously within its walls that I have no doubt
the quaint inmates supposed themselves in their
native haunts.

They chattered and scolded each other, wildly
chased stray little dogs and kittens, and really
seemed to know so much that I half believed an old
keeper, who told me the only reason they did rot

12

talk, was because they could make themselves well enough understood without.

Many funny stories I heard of their sagacity. One I recall of a nurse who shook a naughty little boy in the presence of some of the mother monkeys, whereupon all the old monkeys began shaking all the young ones until it seemed as if their poor little heads would drop off.

But, interested in all the singular inhabitants of the house, I grew attached to Joe, the young chimpanzee who had been brought a baby from the coast of Guinea the winter before. He had a little room on the sunny side of the monkey house, with a stove, table, chairs and a couple of beds arranged like the berths in the state room of an ocean steamer. Besides he had a man all to himself, to wait upon him; and it was no wonder the other monkeys were jealous of his superior quarters and the deference paid him; for while Joe was not handsome he was worth more money than all the others put together.

He was worth this great sum because he belonged to the most intelligent and interesting species of the monkey family, and only one or two of his kinsfolk had ever been seen in Europe, while the only one the Zoological Society had ever owned, had died of lung fever before he had inhabited his comfortable quarters many months.

Joe was about as tall as an average boy of eight or ten years. He wore a thick cloth roundabout, and a low flat trencher cap such as the Oxford students delight in.

One day I walked to the door of his room and knocked. The keeper said "Come in," and as I did so Joe walked erect over the floor to me, pulled off his cap with his left hand, and put out his right to shake mine. When I said "It is a fine morning," he bowed briskly; but when I added, "Are you pretty well, Joe?" he shook his head and looked very sober. The keeper explained: "Joe had a cold, and that made him very low spirited."

Joe was listening attentively; and when the man finished, he shivered and drew up the collar of his jacket round his hairy throat, as if to confirm the statement.

I gave him an apple, which he looked at a moment, then opened the door of the oven of his stove, and put it in out of sight. Seeming to understand that the fire was low, he pulled a basket from under the lower berth and took some bits of wood from it to the stove. Then the keeper handed him a match,

and he lighted a fire as cleverly as any Yankee boy
I ever saw.

"Show the lady how you read *The Times*, Joe,"
said the keeper.

JOE READS "*The Times.*"

Joe drew up a chair, tilted it back a little, spread
his legs apart, opened the sheet, turned it until he
found the page he wanted, then settled himself into
the exact position of the comfortable English gentle-

man who supposes *The Times* is printed for his ex-
clusive use.   It was impossible to help laughing, and
the sly twinkle in his narrow eye assured us Joe himself knew how funny it was.

Quite a crowd had gathered at the open door of
his room, and as he noticed it, he put his hand in his
pocket drew out the one eye-glass Englishman so
particularly affect, and put it to his eye looking as
weakly wise as Lord Dundreary himself.   After a
little he grew tired of so many spectators, left his
chair and quietly shut the door in their faces.

Looking about as if he would do something more
for our amusement, he remembered his apple in the
stove oven.   Running there he took hold of the door,
but suddenly drew back, for it was hot.   He laughed
a little at his discomfiture which he took in good
part, stood thinking a moment, then used his pocket-
handkerchief as deftly as a dainty lady would to ac-
complish his purpose.   But if the door was hot,
the apple, Joe logically reasoned, must be hotter ; so
he ventured not to touch it before opening his knife.
Wondering what he was going to do, I found him
sticking the blade into the apple and bringing it out
in triumph.   The keeper gave him a plate, and after
letting the apple cool a little he offered it to us.   We

courteously declined, but the servant tasted, ex·
plaining that Joe did not like to eat anything alone.
Then Joe followed, but did not like the flavor, and
being asked if it was sour, he nodded. We were

JOE TRIES HIS APPLE.

told that he, in common with the other monkeys,
liked oranges and bananas better than any other
fruits.

Yet he kept tasting a little of the apple from a spoon while the keeper told us how the sailors who hoped to capture his mother only succeeded in bringing him off alive after they had killed her. They had hard work to keep him alive on board ship, but found a warm nook for him by the galley fire. He was in fair health when they landed, so they obtained the large price offered by the Zoological Gardens; but in spite of the most devoted care, he seemed to languish in his new home.

"Do you love me, Joe?" the man ended his story with. Joe nodded, smiled, and put his head lovingly on the other's shoulder.

As we left that day, Joe took his hat, cane, and heavy wrap, and escorted us to the great door of the monkey house, shaking our hands as we bade him good-bye.

Another time when I called he was taking tea, using milk and sugar and handling cup and saucer as if he had been familiar with them from his earliest days. He motioned us to take chairs. We did so and he jumped up, found cups for us, and then passed a plate of biscuits, laughing with glee as we took one. I have taken tea with many curious individuals, but never expect to be so honored again as to be invited by a chimpanzee.

Noticing his hand was feverish, I found his pulse was 130. I said "What is the matter of him?"

"Consumption is what kills all of them," the man answered, low, just as if talking before a human invalid.

From that day Joe failed rapidly, and one morning under the head of "Great Loss," *The Times* announced that he died at midnight.

I went down at once to see the keeper whose grief I knew would be keen.

He told me how for days, Joe could only be persuaded to take food by seeing him eat and hearing him praise it, how he made him sleep in his berth by his side, and when death came, held his hand through all the last struggle.

The man's voice was actually choked with sobs as he said, "It don't seem right, indeed it don't, not to have a funeral for him! He ought to have had it."

I never heard Joe had any funeral, but I did hear that he was stuffed, and looks more like a big boy than when he was alive.

MARKET DAY AT PAU.

IF you don't know where Pau is, do as I did when I first heard of it, — look it up on some large map of France.

Down in the southeast corner, at the mouth of the Adour river, you will see the city from which the bayonet is said to have received its name; and if you move your finger along about an inch due east from Bayonne you will be likely to pass it directly under Pau.

It is the capital of one of the finest departments of France, the Basses-Pyrenees; and its mild, equable climate and charming scenery have made it, for the last thirty years, a favorite winter resort for invalids and pleasure-seekers.

As the capital of the old province of Béarn, and as the seat of the ancient royal castle where flourished

the Gastons and Marguerites, and where Henri IV. of
France was born, Pau has many interesting historical
associations, upon which, however, we must resolutely
turn our backs if we mean to go to market this morning.

Monday is always market-day at Pau, and then it
is that the country comes bodily in and takes possession of the town. At five o'clock in the morning the
rumbling of cart-wheels and the clatter of sabots
down in the cold gray streets announce the approach
of a rustic army from the villages round about. On
they come from every quarter all through the fore-
noon, and if we walk out anywhere — say to the
Allées de Morlaäs, where we can sit on one of the
benches under the trees and gaze now and then at
the distant snowy Pyrenees, — we shall see the end-
less stream of market-people.

The men wear round woolen caps without visors,
called the *béret*; a short frock, usually of some coarse
cotton material, which is gathered so much about the
neck as not to improve their stumpy figures; and
huge wooden shoes that rattle and thump along the
pavements, bringing with them on rainy days an in-
credible quantity of country mud.

The most noticeable feature in the dress of the
women is the bright foulard handkerchief that serves

instead of hat or bonnet. It is arranged according to the taste and age of the wearer, and is capable of producing a wide range of effects.

The guide-book assures us that the *paysannes* walk

A PEASANT WOMAN.

barefoot on the country roads; but, upon approaching the town, they cover their wayworn feet with the cherished shoes and stockings that have thus been spared from wear and tear.

On a cold spring morning we saw a company of women descending a hill at Lourdes with enormous bundles of wood on their heads. As we were pitying the bare feet that went toiling down the steep way, we suddenly spied their shoes dangling from the fagots where they had considerately placed them, to be out of harm.

The strength of these little peasant women is wonderful. They walk off with grand strides, carrying heavy burdens on their heads, and sometimes knitting as they go. Many of the young girls are very pretty; but exposure and hard work soon change the fresh tint and the graceful outlines to a brown wrinkled visage and a gaunt ungainly figure.

Sitting here, we are attracted by a jaunty young creature tripping along with a large, round, shallow basket of salad, or *choux de Bruxelles*, on her head, carelessly steadying it with one hand, while in the other she carries a pair of chickens or a basket of eggs. But how can we see a pinched-looking woman tugging along under a big bag of potatoes, or breaking stones on the road, without feeling tired ourselves and sad? And neither the sadness nor the weariness is lightened upon seeing, as we invariably do, that when a woman is working with a man he generously gives her the heaviest end of the load.

The wood is brought in on clumsy carts, generally two-wheeled and often covered. The oxen and cows that draw these carts have their bodies draped with coarse linen covers, and across their heads is a strip of sheep-skin, which is worn with the shaggy side out

OX-TEAM.

and the skinny side in. M. Taine tells us in his book on the Pyrenees that he saw the heads of the cattle protected by thread nets and ferns, which, I trust is their usual summer coiffure ; for in a country where, in winter, gentlemen carry parasols and wear large white streamers depending from their hats, to protect the head and back of the neck from the too ardent rays of the sun, even the " patient ox " might complain of the unfitness of a head-dress of sheep skin.

The driver of the ox-team is armed with a long stick, at the end of which is an iron goad. This he uses either in guiding the cattle, which is done by going in advance of them and stretching the stick backward with a queer, stiff gesture, or in pricking and prodding the poor creatures till they hardly know which way to turn. The cattle, which are mostly of a light brown color, are very large and fine ; but it seems strange to us to see cows wearing the yoke.

But, O! the donkey! The wise, the tough, the musical, the irresistible, the universal donkey! How shall I ever give you an idea of what he becomes to an appreciative mind that has daily opportunities of studying his "tricks and manners!"

Fancy one of these long-eared, solemn-eyed gentry, scarcely larger than a good-sized Newfoundland dog jogging along with a double pannier bulging at his sides and a fat market-woman on his back.

But the disproportion between the size of the beast and that of his burden, and his gravity and circumspection, is scarcely funnier here than when he is placed before a two-wheeled cart, a story and a half higher than himself, and containing a man, a woman, a boy, and a pig ; sometimes cabbages and chickens, often two or three inexperienced calves. And in the afternoon, when market is over, I have often seen six or seven women huddled into one of these primitive chariots, each provided with the inevitable stocking

"ONE OF THESE LONG-EARED, SOLEMN-EYED GENTRY."

her tongue and her knitting-needles keeping time as the cart goes tilting along over the famous roads of the Basses-Pyrénées. The gay handkerchiefs of the women, the purple, blue and gray stockings with their flashing needles, and the huge brown loaves of bread sure to be protruding in various quarters, made these groups, returning from market, most pictur-esquely striking.

Coming in from the *Allées de Morlaäs* we find, as we approach the *Place des Ecoles*, an animated scene. The broad sidewalk is lined with rows of women sell-ing vegetables, fruit, flowers, poultry and eggs. The haggling of the buyers and the gibing of the venders, though carried on in *patois* unintelligible to us, are expressed in tones and accompanied by gestures that translate them quite effectively ; especially as not a market-day passes without a long recital from our Catherine, illustrating the greed of the peasants and her own superior finesse.

" How much do you want for this chicken ? "

" Three francs."

" Keep your chicken for somebody see.   I'll go to another."

" Stay !   What will you give for it ? "

" Two francs."

" Get along with you ! "

As Catherine eyes the chicken which she secretly admires and openly abuses, another cook comes up and lays her hand on its comely breast.   It is a deci-sive moment, but Catherine is equal to the emer-gency.

" Stand off there !   I'm here first."

Then, with a secret resolve that her *demoiselles* shall dine on that little plump *poulet,* she offers fifty sous and carries off the prize. To see her enter our *salon* bearing a waiter on which are a dozen fine rosy apples and two large russet pears, with the question, "Guess how much I paid for all?" written in every line of her shrewd old face, is something worth coming to Europe for. To make a sharp bargain, to cook a good dinner, and never to waste anything, these are the aims of her life and the themes of her discourse.

Our snug *appartement* is opposite the *Place des Efoles,* where the wood and cattle are sold; and the first peep in the morning gives us a picture, lively enough and foreign enough to make us look and look again many times during the day, till late in the afternoon when the *Place* is nearly bare; and the aspect of the few patient but rather dejected-looking peasants whose wood has not yet found purchasers almost tempts us to run over and buy a load or two, just for the pleasure of sending the poor creatures home with lighter hearts and heavier pockets. What would Catherine say to that, I wonder?

Besides the interest which we feel in the various natural hangers-on of the wood-carts (and each one has from two to five of both sexes and all sizes), we

13

"THE FAVORITE WAY OF TRANSPORTING A PIG."

get no small amusement from their patrons, who represent all sorts of townspeople, from the fat old woman of the green grocery and sausage-shop over the way, who peddles with easy affability among the market-people, to the lordly young Englishman who dashes on to the *Place* with the air of a conquering hero, and loftily indicates with his riding-whip the load that has the honor to meet his approval.

Troops of frisky calves are scattered about, and groups of blue blouses and red *bérets* are earnestly discussing the merits of the unsuspecting innocents. More rarely a fine cow, or a yoke of oxen, attracts a circle of connoisseurs; then the *patois* becomes more fluent, and the gestures more animated, and the fists of the interested parties are seen flourishing unpleasantly near the disdainful noses of the critics.

The prolonged and penetrating squeal of that pig in the *Rue des Cultivateurs* reminds me that this interesting animal figures largely in the scenes of market-day. Pork being an important article of peasant diet, Mr. Piggy is always abroad on Monday and contributes largely to the general éclat.

The favorite way of transporting a moderate sized pig is to put him about the neck, holding his hind feet with one hand and his forefeet with the other. This method, though attended with some disadvantages, such as the proximity of the squeal to the ear of the carrier, is, on the whole, less worrying than that of tying a string to one of the hind legs of his Porkship, this giving him a chance to pull his way with more or less effect, while the peasant is frantically jerking in the opposite direction.

Not infrequently a pig gets a ride home from market in the cart of his new owner. Then, true to his nature and principles, he resists the honor accorded him with the whole might of his legs and lungs; so that, with a man at his hind legs, a woman at his left ear, and a boy at his right fore leg, he is with difficulty assisted to his coach and is held there, *en route,* by that " eternal vigilance " which is, in more senses than one, " the price of liberty."

On the *Rue Porte Neuve* and near the *Halle Neuve,* in the centre of the town, the venders of agricultural implements, kitchen hardware, locks and keys, second-

"A GRAY-HAIRED SPINNER WITH HER ANCIENT DISTAFF."

hand books, handkerchiefs, collars, cuffs, hats, bracelets, rings, baskets, brooms, bottles, mouse-traps, and other miscellaneous articles, display their goods, and a sudden shower makes bad work in this busy community.

By the *Halle Neuve* is the fruit and vegetable market also, and farther on, in the *Rue de la Préfecture,* we suddenly come upon a hollow square inclosed on three sides by ancient looking buildings, one of which is the *Vieille Halle*; and here are fish, poultry and game, and the queerest-looking market-people in the whole town, it seems to me.

There is a flower market on the *Place Royal,* and you will see the Spanish women there, with their foulards and trinkets, to catch a few sous from the rustics.

We cannot confine our interest to the market-folk, however, for everybody is more or less picturesque in this strange land, and we are never tired of saying, "See here," and "See there." Sometimes it is a gray-haired spinner with her ancient distaff that attracts our notice, as she sits in a sunny door-way or totters along the sidewalk ; and then there are the antics of these foreign children I Béarnais boys are as fond of standing on their heads as their American brethren are, but their large and heavy *sabots* are a great in convenience.

Just look at those wooden shoes ranged along the sidewalk over there, while the owners thereof are flourishing their emancipated heels in fine style.

These are some of the sights of a market-day at

Pau; but how can you ever get a notion of the sounds? For when we add to the market-day hub-bub the various every-day street cries that mingle

"As fond of standing on their heads as their American brethren."

with it we have a strange orchestra.

There are the charcoal men, who begin on a high key and drop with an almost impossible interval to a prolonged, nasal, twanging note; the old clo' men, whose *patois* for rags sounds so exactly like my com-

panion's name that she is sure they are after the
dresses she is economically wearing out at Pau ; the
chimney-sweeps ; the *jonchée* women, who sell cream
cheese, rolled in what looks like onion-tops; the
roasted chestnut women, whose shrill " Tookow ! "
(*patois* for " *Tout chaud* ") suggests piping-hot chest-
nuts in bursting shells ; and the crockery and earthen
men, who push their wares before them in long shallow box-carts, and give, in a sustained recitative, the
whole catalogue of delf and pottery.

In the afternoon when the noise and stir are sub-
siding, we hear a few notes, often repeated, from
what I should like to call a shepherd's pipe ; only the
instrument in question is not in the least like one,
but resembles more one of those little musical toys
with a row of holes cut along one side, upon which
our children at home are so fond of performing.
However, our shepherd contrives to produce a pasto-
ral effect with his simple strain, and we favor the illusion of the pipe by only listening to him, while we
look at his pretty goats with long, silky black hair.
He leads them through the town twice a day, and at
the sound of his call those who wish goat's milk send
out their glasses and get it warm from a goat milked
at the door. As his last faint notes die out in the
distance the rosy light fades from the peaks of the
Pyrenees ; the sun has set, and market-day is over.

IL SANTISSIMO BAMBINO.

O N the Capitoline Hill, in Rome, stands a church, twelve hundred years old, called Ara Cœli. It is unpromising in its outward appearance, but is rich in marbles and mosaics within.

The most precious possession of this ancient church however, is a wooden doll called Il Santissimo Bambino — The Most Holy Infant. It is dressed like an Italian baby, and an Italian baby is dressed like a mummy. We often see them in their mothers' arms, so swathed that they can no more move than a bundle without any baby inside of it. Their little legs must ache for the freedom of kicking. The dress of *the* Bambino is very different from that of *a* bambino after all, for it is cloth of silver, and it sparkles all over with jewels which have been presented to it, and it wears a golden crown upon its head.

This is the history of this remarkable doll, as devout

Roman Catholics believe. You must judge for your-
selves how much of it is truth and how much fable.

They say this image of the infant Saviour was
carved from olive-wood which grew upon the Mount
of Olives, by a monk who lived in Palestine; and, as
he had no means of painting it with sufficient beauty,
his prayers prevailed upon St. Luke to come down
from Heaven and color it for him. Then he sent it to
Rome to be present at the Christmas festival. It was
shipwrecked on the way, but finally came safely to
land, and was received with great reverence by the
Franciscan monks, who placed it in a shrine at Ara
Cœli. It was soon found to have miraculous power
to heal the sick, and was so often sent for to visit
them, that, at one time, it received more fees than any
physician in Rome. It has its own carriage in which
it rides abroad, and its own attendants who guard it
with the utmost care.

One woman was so selfish as to think it would be
a capital thing if she could get possession of this won-
der-working image for herself and her friends.

"She had another doll prepared of the same size
and appearance as the 'Santissimo,' and having
feigned sickness and obtained permission to have it
left with her, she dressed the false image in its
clothes, and sent it back to Ara Cœli. The fraud was

THE BAMBINO.

not discovered till night, when the Franciscan monks were awakened by the most furious ringing of bells and by thundering knocks at the west door of the church, and, hastening thither, could see nothing but a wee, naked, pink foot peeping in from under the door; but when they opened the door, without stood the little naked figure of the true Bambino of Ara Cœli, shivering in the wind and rain. So the false baby was sent back in disgrace, and the real baby restored to its home, never to be trusted away alone any more."

This marvelous escape is duly recorded in the Sacristy of the church where the Bambino safely dwells under lock and key all the year, except the time from Christmas to Epiphany, when it comes out to receive the homage of the people.

We went to see it last Christmas.

As I told you, the church stands on one of the Seven Hills of the Eternal City; it is approached by a flight of stone steps as wide as the building itself and as high as the hill. There were many beggars on these steps; some old and blind, others young and bright-eyed. Beside the beggars, there were people with tiny images of the Baby in the Manger, toy sheep, and pictures of the Bambino for sale.

When we went into the church, we found one of the

chapels fitted up like a tableau. The chapels are something like large alcoves along the sides of a church. Each is consecrated to some saint, and often belongs to some particular family who have their weddings and funerals there.

It was in the second chapel on the left that we found the scene represented. The Virgin Mary was dressed in a bright blue silk, adorned with various jewels. In her lap lay the Bambino, about the size of a baby six weeks old. I do not believe St. Luke painted its face, for it was not half so well done as most of the wooden dolls we see. An artificial mule had his nose close to the baby's head. Joseph sat near, and in front the shepherds were kneeling. All these people were of life-size, made of wood, and dressed in real clothes. Beyond them was to be seen a pretty landscape — sheep, covered with real wool, a girl with a pitcher on her head coming down a path to a sparkling fountain of *glass*. In the distance was the town of Bethlehem. In mid-air hovered an angel, hung by a wire in his back from the ceiling. On pasteboard screens, above the Virgin and Child were painted a crowd of cherubs looking down, and in their midst God the Father — whom no one hath seen nor can see — was represented in the likeness of a venerable man, spreading his hands in blessing over the group below.

THE EQUIPAGE OF THE BAMBINO.

A great many little children were coming with the older people to look at all this, and talking, in their pretty Italian tongue, about the "Bambino."

Epiphany, as perhaps you know, is the day kept in memory of the visit of the Wise Men where the Star in the East guided to our Saviour's cradle. On that day, Il Santissimo Bambino was to be carried with all ceremony back to the Sacristy; so we went to see that.

We were glad to find the Blessed Virgin had two nice silk dresses; she had changed from blue to red, and the Bambino was standing on her knee. The Shepherds had gone, and the Wise Men had come, all very gorgeous in flowered brocade and cloth of gold, with crowns on their heads, and pages to hold their trains.

It was yet an hour or two before the " Procession of the Bambino" would proceed; so we went out of the side door of the church to stray about the Capitoline Hill in the meanwhile.

We went down the steps where Tiberias Gracchus, the friend of the people, was killed, some two thousand years ago. That brought us into a small square called Piazza di Campidoglio. It is surrounded on three sides by public buildings, and in front has a grand stairway leading down to the street. It was in this very spot that Brutus made his famous speech after the assassination of Julius Cæsar. We crossed the square, went up some steps and through an archway.

A company of little Romans were playing soldier there, and the small drum-major made the walls of the capitol resound with his rattling music. That reminds me to tell you that Santa Claus does not visit Italy; but an old woman, named Navona, comes instead. She may be his wife, for aught I know; in fact, it seems quite likely, for she has a way, just like his, of coming down the chimney, bringing gifts for the good children and switches for the naughty. These must have been very good little boys, for every one of them seemed to have a new sword or gun. Probably Navona has to keep the house while Santa Claus is away about his Christmas business, and that is the reason she does not reach her small people here until the night before Epiphany, the 6th of January.

We went down a lane of poor houses, dodging the clothes which hung drying over our heads, and came to a large green gate in the high stone wall of a garden. We knocked, but no one answered. Presently a black-eyed little boy came running to us, glad to earn two or three sous by going to call the *custode.* While we wait for him to do so, I must tell you why

14

we wished to go through this green door. You have read, either in Latin or English, the story of Tarpæia, the Roman maiden, who consented to show the Latin soldiers the way into the citadel if they would give her what they wore on their left arms, meaning their bracelets, and then the grim joke they played after she had done her part, by throwing upon her their shields, which were also "what they wore on their left arms."

It was to see the Tarpæian rock, where she led her country's enemies up, and where, later, traitors were hurled down, that we wished to go through the gate. Presently the keeper came, a rosy young woman, leading a little girl, who was feeling very rich over a new dolly she was dangling by its arm.

We were admitted to a small garden, where pretty pink roses were in blossom, and the oranges were hanging on the trees, though the icicles were fringing the fountain not far away. On the edge of the garden, along the brow of the cliff, runs a thick wall of brown stone; we leaned over it and looked down the steep rock which one assaulting party after another tried, in old times, to scale.

It was on this side that the Gauls were trying to reach the citadel at the time the geese saved the city Do you know that for a loñg time, annually, a dog was crucified on the capitol, and a goose carried in triumph, because, on that occasion, the dogs failed to give the alarm and the geese did it!

We looked down on the roofs and into the courts of poor houses which have huddled close about the foot of the hill, but beyond them we could look down into the Forum, where Virginia was stabbed, where Horatius hung up the spoil of the Curiatii, where the body of Julius Cæsar was burned, where the head of Cicero was cruelly exposed on the very rostrum where had often been seen the triumph of his eloquence. Opposite to us stood the Palatine Hill, a mass of crumbling palaces; a little farther off rose the mighty wall of the Coliseum, where the gladiators used to fight, and where so many Christian martyrs were thrown to the wild beasts while tens of thousands of their fellow-men, more cruel than lions, looked on, for sport.

Just at the roots of the Capitoline, close by, though out of sight, was the Mamertine Prison, where St. Paul, of whom the world was not worthy, was once shut up in the dismal darkness of the dungeon.

As we went from the garden back to the Piazza di Campidoglio, we saw something unusual was going on in the palace on the left of the capital. In the door stood a guard in resplendent array of crim-

FAMILY OF ROMAN BEGGARS.

son and gold lace. Looking through the arched entrance, we could see in the inner court an open carriage
with driver and footman in livery of bright scarlet.
Something of a crowd was gathering in the corridors.
We stopped to learn what it was all about. An Italian
woman answered, " La Principessa Margarita ! " and
an English lady close by explained that the Princess
Margaret, wife of the crown prince, had come to dis-
tribute prizes to the children of the public schools.
Only invited guests could be present, but the people
were waiting to see her come down. So we joined the
people and waited also.

It was a long time and a pretty cold one. A brass
band in the court cheered our spirits now and then.
The fine span of the princess looked rather excited, at
first, by the trumpets so close to their ears, but they
stood their ground bravely. If one of the scarlet
footmen tightened a buckle, it raised our hopes that
his mistress was coming ; the other put a fresh cigar
in his mouth, and they sank.

Meantime the guard in the gold-laced crimson coat
and yellow silk stockings paced up and down. At
length there was a messenger from above ; the royal
carriage drove under the arch close to us. There was
a rustle, and down came the princely lady, dressed in
purple velvet, with mauve feathers in her hat, a white

veil drawn over her face, and a large bouquet in her white-gloved hand — rather pretty, and very graceful. Before entering her carriage, she turned to shake hands with the ladies and gentlemen who had accompanied her. She was very complaisant, bowing low to them, and they still lower to her. Then she bowed graciously to the crowd right and left, and they responded gratefully. She smiled upon them, high and low, but there was a look in her face, as it passed close to me, as if she was tired of smiling for the public. She seated herself in the carriage ; the lady-in-waiting took her place beside her, the gentleman-in-waiting threw over them the carriage-robe of white ermine lined with light blue velvet and stepped in himself.

Then the equipage rolled off, the scarlet footmen getting up behind as it started. This princess is very good and kind, greatly beloved by the people, and, as there is no queen, she is the first lady in the kingdom. Her husband first and her little son next are heirs to the crown.

This show being over, we hastened back to the church, fearing we had missed the Bambino in our pursuit of the princess. But we were in good time. On the side of the church opposite the tableau was a small, temporary platform. Little boys and girls were placed upon this, one after the other, to speak short pieces or recite verses about the Infant Christ. It was a kind of Sunday-school concert in Italian. The language is very sweet in a child's mouth. There were a great many bright, black-eyed children in the church, and most of them seemed to have brought their Christmas presents along with them, as if to show them to the Bambino.

There were ragged men in the crowd, and monks, and country-women with handkerchiefs tied over their heads for bonnets. One of them who stood near me had her first finger covered with rings up to the last joint. That is their great ambition in the way of dress.

At length the organ ceased playing, and the notes of a military band were heard. Then we saw a banner moving slowly down one of the aisles, followed by a train of lighted tapers. Over the heads of the people we could only see the banner and the lights ; they passed down and paused to take the Bambino. Then they marched slowly all around the church — people falling on their knees as they passed by.

Out at the front door they went, and that sacred image was held high aloft, so that all the people on the great stairway and in the square below might get a sight of it, and be blessed. Then up the middle of the church they came, to the high altar. This was our chance to see them perfectly.

First the banner with the image of the Virgin on it

was borne by a young priest dressed in a long black robe and a white short gown trimmed with lace ; next came a long procession of men in ordinary dress, carrying long and large wax candles, which they had a disagreeable habit of dripping as they went along.

"Servants of great houses," remarked a lady behind me.

"They used to come themselves," answered another.

Then followed Franciscan monks in their brown copes, each with a knotted rope for a girdle, and sandals only on his bare feet. After these came the band of musicians, all little boys; and now approached, with measured tread, three priests in rich robes of white brocade, enriched with silver. The middle one, a tall, venerable-looking man, with hoary hair and solemn countenance, held erect in his hands the sacred dolly. As it passed, believers dropped upon their knees. When he reached the high altar, he reverently kissed its feet, and delivered it to its custodian to be carried to the Sacristy!

www.ingramcontent.com/pod-product-compliance
Lightning Source LLC
Chambersburg PA
CBHW022146020726
47496CB00008B/2574